700

This LITTLE MAMMOTH belongs to

_____

_____

_____

DILLY'S

BIRTHDAY PARTY

DILLY'S
BIRTHDAY PARTY

by
Tony Bradman

illustrated by
Susan Hellard

LITTLE
MAMMOTH

'Come on, Father,' said Dilly. '*Let's go!*'
Dilly was *so* excited. His best friend Dixie was having
a birthday party, and Dilly couldn't wait to get there.
'Just behave yourself this time, Dilly,' said Father.
'Dixie won't want her party spoilt by a naughty
little dinosaur.'
Dilly promised to be good. Dorla snorted.

When they arrived, Dixie's mother asked Dorla to stay.
'I think I'll need all the help I can get,' she said.
'I'll help too!' said Dilly. Everyone laughed.
'You just concentrate on enjoying yourself, Dilly,'
said Dixie's mother.
'He certainly knows how to do *that*,' said Father.

Dilly and Dorla took off their coats. Suddenly there was a pounding on the door. Dixie's mother opened it. 'Yippee!' shouted the small dinosaur who burst in. 'It's . . . PARTY TIME!'
'You haven't met Dudley before, have you, Dilly?' said Dixie's mother. 'He's very . . . er, lively.'

'Happy birthday, Dixie!' said Dilly. 'Wait till you see the present I got for you. It's terrific!'

But before Dixie could take the present, Dudley pushed
Dilly out of the way.
'Open mine first, Dixie!' said Dudley. 'It's much
better than *that* one.'

'How about some party games now?' said Dixie's mother.
'I thought we could start with Pass The Fern Leaf.'

Dorla was in charge of the music. The little
dinosaurs sat in a circle and passed the fern leaf
round. But when the music stopped, Dudley grabbed it
from Dilly.
'I'm the winner!' he shouted. Dilly just scowled.

Next they played Musical Dinosaurs . . . then Dead
Lizards . . . and Follow-My-Tail.

Dudley won every time. There was just no stopping him.
'Please don't do that, Dudley,' said Dixie's mother.
But Dudley took no notice.
Dorla was beginning to wish she hadn't stayed to help.

Soon all the other little dinosaurs were *very* excited and *very* noisy.

At last it was time for them to sit at the table.
Everyone sang Happy Birthday to Dixie.
'Blow out the candles, Dixie!' said her mother.
'Then you can make a wish!'
But Dudley blew them out first. Dixie burst into tears.
'I've never been *that* naughty,' Dilly whispered.

'I think it's time you all let off some steam in the garden,' said Dixie's mother. 'Maybe that will calm you down a little.'
But it didn't. Dudley and the others went absolutely *crazy*.

'Oh no,' said Dixie's mother. 'This is getting out of hand. But what can we do to stop them?'
Dilly smiled. Dorla knew what was coming next.

Dilly opened his mouth . . . and blasted off an ultra-special, 150-mile-per-hour super-scream, the kind that makes everyone freeze in their tracks and clamp their paws over their ears. Dilly stopped screaming at last.

Dorla noticed that now Dudley was staring at Dilly
in utter amazement.
After that, everyone was *much* better behaved.
'Er . . . thank you, Dilly,' said Dixie's mother.
'That's all right,' said Dilly, proudly. Then Dudley
came over. He wanted Dilly to teach *him* how to scream.
'I think we'll stick to quiet games now, Dudley,'
said Dixie's mother quickly.

Later, Father came to pick them up. Dixie's mother
said both Dorla *and* Dilly had been very helpful. She
gave them a special party bag each. Dilly was really
pleased.
'Oh, wow!' he said. 'I can't wait till Dixie's party
next year!'
'I certainly can,' said Dixie's mother. And they all
laughed!

First published in Great Britain 1991
by Piccadilly Press Ltd
Published 1993 by Little Mammoth
an imprint of Reed Consumer Books Ltd
Michelin House, 81 Fulham Road, London SW3 6RB
and Auckland, Melbourne, Singapore and Toronto

Text copyright © Tony Bradman, 1991
Illustrations copyright © Susan Hellard, 1991

The right of Tony Bradman to be identified as Author and
Susan Hellard to be identified as Illustrator of this
work has been asserted by them in accordance with the
Copyright Designs and Patent Act, 1988

ISBN 0 7497 1189 2

A CIP catalogue record for this title
is available at the British Library

Printed in Great Britain
by Scotprint Ltd., Musselburgh